The Little Librarians & The Key To Kindness

Written by Jasmine McLean

Illustrated by Joanna Maria

Grosvenor House
Publishing Limited

This book is published by
Grosvenor House Publishing Ltd
Link House
140 The Broadway, Tolworth, Surrey, KT6 7HT.
www.grosvenorhousepublishing.co.uk

This book is a work of fiction. Any resemblance to
people or events, past or present, is purely coincidental.

A CIP record for this book
is available from the British Library

ISBN 978-1-83975-578-1

This book belongs to.......................

For Imaani and Soraya.

May you always give and receive kindness.

Not forgetting the ultimate King of Kindness - Michael McLean.

It's **nice** to be **kind,**

and it's **kind** to be **nice.**

We can be kind with our
words.

We can be kind with a
surprise.

Someone will always remember how we made them **feel.**

We can bake them a delicious cake or **share** our yummy meal.

Kindness can be listening

or it can be singing a happy song.

Kindness can be telling someone
they are right
or maybe if they are wrong.

Kindness can be found absolutely anywhere.

It can be in **cuddles** with
our loved ones or offering our chair.

Kindness can be for **all different faces** and

kindness can be from **all different places.**

It can be when we say, 'Hello'

to someone or ask them,

'How are you?'

It can be when we help someone to understand something, and they can help us too!

Kindness isn't just for **humans,**

be they little or tall.

Kindness is **caring** for all creatures,

be they
great

or small.

TO SAVE

When we **care** for all the **animals**, insects, plants and **trees**,

and when we care for

all the **mammals** across

the **oceans** and

the **seas,**

Love can travel through the universe like a magical, summer breeze.

Kindness leads to love and love leads to healing.

Being kind, without a doubt, is such a lovely feeling.

Kindness isn't just for others,

it's for **yourself** too.

As well as caring for the world,

you have to **care for you!**

Let's think more about kindness...

What types of behaviour can be 'Kind' behaviour?

What sort of gifts can you give to make someone smile?

How can you be kind to animals, plants and trees?

Why is it important to look after the Ocean?

How can saying, "Hello" to someone or asking, "How are you?" make them feel?

What are the types of things you can do to be kind to yourself?

What song makes you feel happy?

Who do you know that could use a
little kindness and what would you like
to do for them?

The next activity is a colouring one.

Now let's colour in the big letters,

to make the message loud and clear.

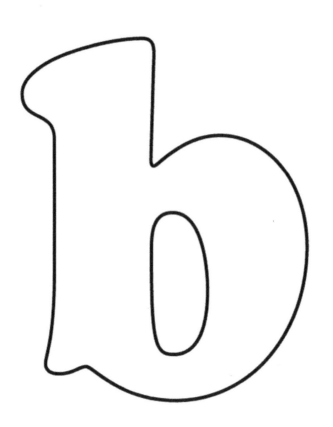

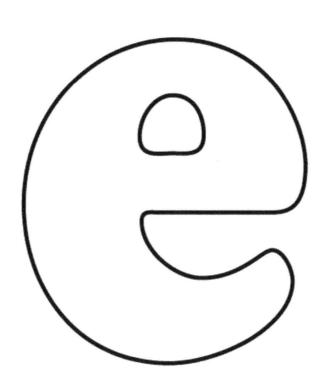

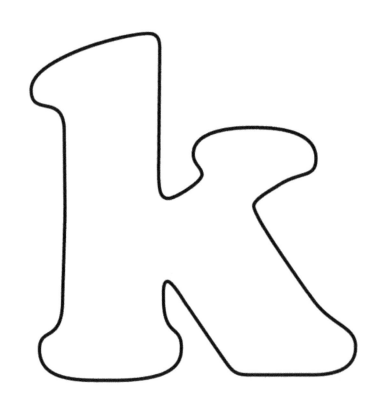

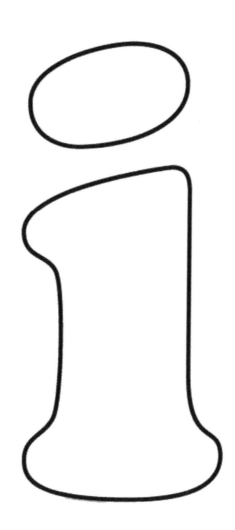

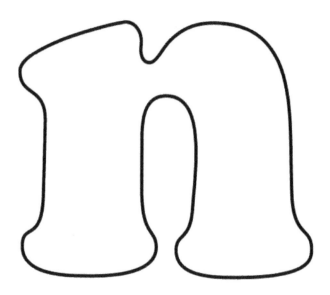

About the author

Proud mum and passionate reader, Jasmine wanted to share her love of books with her children to give them the opportunity to enjoy the magic that reading brings...and so @ The_Little_Librarian's Instagram page was born.

As any adult in the position of nurturing a child will know, teaching children about important core values can be quite a daunting task...but she wanted to place this message of kindness and love into the universe as a tool for other families and educational establishments to share with the little readers of the future.

Teaching children about kindness from a young age and the impact it has will change the world.

Acknowledgements

Thank you to everyone who answered their phone and took the time out to share their thoughts and feedback on this little piece.

A special shout to Rebecca at GHP for being so patient and helpful when she had an email or me on the phone every other day!

Thank you to Romel and Ellia who offered the most incredible feedback and really shared their honest thoughts to help me get this right! Some of those phone calls took place at midnight when all our kids were asleep, I am very grateful for your time.

Thank you to Joanna Maria, an incredible artist and old school friend! So honoured to have worked with someone so talented to bring the message to life.

Finally thank you to my lovely family who were the first people to teach me all about kindness!

CPSIA information can be obtained
at www.ICGtesting.com
Printed in the USA
BVHW020253051021
618136BV00010B/195

9 781839 755781